AF406589

Porcelain Jade's Escape

Stacey Williams

Published by Stacey Williams, 2022.

This is a work of fiction. Similarities to real people, places, or events are entirely coincidental.

PORCELAIN JADE'S ESCAPE

First edition. August 16, 2022.

Copyright © 2022 Stacey Williams.

ISBN: 979-8201484262

Written by Stacey Williams.

Thank you my friends, family and fans for believing in me to give you a good story.

PREFACE

Jade let everybody believe her life was over, but in reality, it had just begun. She said what she needed to say to Diane while she was on the rollers ready to go into the fire. There was a fifty-fifty chance it would even work, but Jade rigged the crematorium, hoping it would. What it looked like from Diane's point of view was Jade burning as she listened to her scream. What really happened was; the hopper doors opened, Jade was rolled inside and instantly the burning slab tilted sideways rolling Jade off into the basement, when it tilted back into place there was a porcelain dummy laying down giving Diane the illusion that she was burning. Jade had mats down there to catch her fall. She also had a first aid kit, blankets, snacks and water, enough for a few days and a bucket for bathroom use. She wasn't sure how long she would be down there and needed to be prepared. The sweat Diane saw rolling off Jade's face and arms was not sweat at all but, fire-retardant gel and the clothes she was wearing was sprayed with fire-resistant spray. Jade knew this was a long shot but she had nothing to lose and she knew she would get burned in the process. She landed on the mats and kept rolling to put out any smolder. She pulled out her first aid kit and checked a mirror to see if anything was burned bad enough that needed attention. Surprisingly, her face was not touched but her arms and hands got a little bit along with a few spots on her clothes. Some of her hair was singed but not enough to tell it was missing. She laughed quietly for she knew she had just pulled off Houdini.

Jade laid down below for a while. She could hear muffling above and knew it wasn't safe to come out. It was very dark where she was, the only light she received was coming through a crack in the concrete. She was in an 8x8 space with nothing but 4-foot cement walls around. She didn't want to use her flashlight in case anybody would see a light shining through. She couldn't see much through the cracked concrete except the old car that was in the yard parked under a tree and feet, a lot of feet scurrying around. The only thing she could do while waiting it out was ponder her plan. And it all started when she was nine when the curiosity of what was written in the book her mother had, caught her attention.

~ ONE ~

DEBBIE'S JOURNAL ENTRIES

Jade was nine and her mother didn't come in to kiss her goodnight so she could get a good night's rest before school the next morning. Jade got out of her bed and walked to her mother's room where she peeked through the slightly opened door only to see her mother propped up with pillows on her bed writing in a journal. She had her glasses on so she could see and read. Her mother closed the book with pen inside when Jade walked through the door and asked; "Fancy, what are you doing out of bed?"

"I was waiting for you to come tuck me in, but you never came, so I thought I would come kiss you goodnight."

Debbie held her arms out to give goodnight hugs and kisses. Jade climbed up on the bed next to her mom.

"What are you writing in that book?' She asked.

"I am just writing down my thoughts and feelings in this journal. Secrets really."

"Can I read your journal?"

"Sweetheart, what I write in this journal you wouldn't understand and I don't want you to worry about it. Here is an extra hug and kiss, now go off to bed."

Jade remembered reading what was written in the journal from that night but what surprised her more was this wasn't the first page her mother had written, so Jade started from the very beginning.

January 2, 1978

Diane and I went skiing. We weren't looking for anything to happen this day but something did. We stopped off at the lobby to get some hot cocoa. Once I paid, I turned around to get out of the line and a very cute guy standing behind me (a little too close I might add) bumped right into me spilling my cocoa all down the front of his jacket. He seemed a little angry, but I apologized to him. I told him not to stand so close and he might not get spilled on. I gave him some napkins and I walked away. He came to apologize to me for being a jerk but he was talking to Diane instead. I think he thought she was me. I think this is love at first sight.

PORCELAIN JADE'S ESCAPE

January 11, 1978

Nick asked me out to dinner. He knew it was my birthday. He gave me skiing gloves and two skiing passes. I like him a lot. I turned eighteen. He is two years older than me.

October 28, 1978

A lot of days and months have gone by. I have been seeing Nick a lot. One time in the beginning of our relationship I didn't feel well so I talked Diane into going out with him to a movie. But this date the 28th, Nick took me to his Park City home and proposed to me through an already carved pumpkin. I said yes and couldn't wait to be his wife.

PORCELAIN JADE'S ESCAPE

November 25, 1978

Nick's parents came to Utah. We had a wonderful Thanksgiving meal together. I am not sure how well they like me, but I love their son. Maybe I am not good enough for him.

December 25, 1978

Our first Christmas together. We didn't get each other much but things we could do together like skiing, dinner and movie passes. We enjoy doing these things together.

PORCELAIN JADE'S ESCAPE

December 31, 1978

I have been with Nick almost a year and in a couple months I will be his wife. Happy New Year! So much to plan and do still, but it is coming along.

January 11, 1979

My birthday again and what a day it is. I didn't get my period. I went to the store and bought a test and sure enough, yep, I'm pregnant. I'm only nineteen what am I going to do? How am I going to tell Nick, and his parents? When will I tell Diane?

January 13, 1979

Nick and I got in a huge fight. He told me he wanted to call off the wedding. Was he falling out of love with me? Was I not good enough for him? I told him I was pregnant and he ignored me for three days. When he came back on the sixteenth, he said he was happy and couldn't wait to marry me, but there was something different about him, like he wasn't telling the truth.

February 8, 1979

I got the news my Daddy died today. I don't even know how to take all this in, I am so sad. I am supposed to be married in two days and now I will have to postpone it. Why daddy did you have to die. I wanted you to walk me down the aisle. I wanted you to kiss your daughter on the cheek when you gave my hand to Nick. I am going to miss you so much. I love you, Daddy. Rest in peace.

February 10, 1979

I was supposed to get married today, but it got postponed. I have been juggling the planning between a wedding and a funeral. Diane has been a huge help in all of this. I don't think Nick knows how to show any emotion.

February 12, 1979

Today we buried my father. I am going to miss him. The funeral was short and sweet. My eyes are swollen and my emotions and hormones are out of whack. I cannot believe he is gone. I will now have to make different arrangements for the wedding. I love you, Daddy. I already miss you.

PORCELAIN JADE'S ESCAPE

February 24, 1979

The day of our wedding. Everything was perfect except my father wasn't present. Nick's parents were there, (why would they not be). They are absent parents, making Nick a very spoiled person. I really wasn't sure if they would come. They also live in Europe and that is a long way to travel. I wasn't sure if Nick was going to go through with it, but he did. He seemed more scared than I was. Our honeymoon was very romantic. His parents bought an all-expense paid trip to Hawaii. The beach was most beautiful. The sunsets were divine. The whole thing was magical.

March 15, 1979

I was cramping today. I had a doctor's visit only to find no heartbeat. I was devastated. I couldn't stop crying. I think I cried less at my father's funeral. Nick came with me and held my hand but he didn't show much emotion. We had another checkup a couple weeks later to see how things were going with my body and the doctor had discovered that there might be a chance I will never be able to have kids again. I feel my husband slipping away. The honeymoon is over and it is just a husband-and-wife regular kind of day...everyday! Nick would go to school to finish his Bachelors and then off to work, getting home late.

June 8, 1979

Nicholas graduated from the University of Utah today. He already has a job lined up for him. I am very proud of him for accomplishing this important goal. His parents came to his graduation. One thing to mark off the list of demands they had for him. They gave him a check for $50,000. I've never seen that kind of money, but their promise was real. I wish I got the same time and attention that he put into his schooling. He had already told his parents I lost the baby. I thought they would look at me weird. His mom gave me a hug and told me she was very sorry, but then asked if I was really pregnant in the first place. That hurt. I started to cry. She walked away. Nick actually asked what was wrong but he never confronted his mother about it. I feel so alone.

Time went on and Debbie didn't write much in her journal for eight months. She coped the best she could with the loss of her father and her child and the fact that she didn't know where she fit in exactly. She was lost. She really needed Nick to help her through her heartache and sad times, but she figured she needed to get over it, the best way she could. She turned to her sister for the pain of her father's passing, but never mentioned her own personal loss. They would laugh about past times and tell stories till late in the night.

February 14, 1980

Today is Valentine's Day and I haven't seen Nick. He left for work early in the morning but has not come home yet and it is nearing 6 o'clock. Did he forget what today was, or was it just another day being married to me? I phoned him and surprisingly he answered, but he told me he has to work late. It wasn't like we made plans to go out but it would have been nice to be with him on this occasion, since last year was around the funeral of my father. Why am I here still?

February 20, 1980

Nick is working late yet again. This has become a habit. I am sitting here alone wondering where my husband is and that is the same excuse, he gives me. I wonder if he is with another woman. He hasn't touched me in months. I would like to try and have another child but he doesn't seem interested in me anymore. What did I do so wrong to not be loved?

PORCELAIN JADE'S ESCAPE

February 23, 1980

He is not home again tonight, but he always comes home. I don't know what to think. Last time he came home late we got in an argument and words were said in anger, but I think he personally meant to hurt me. He told me he was thinking about calling off our wedding but then I told him I was pregnant. He told his parents the news and they ultimately made him marry me and told him if he doesn't stay with me, they would not be giving him an inheritance. That was supposed to mean when they die, I thought, but they have been giving him money to pay our expenses and the money he made by supposedly working, he spends at the bar or wherever else he might go.

February 24, 1980

We made it a year. I wish I could say our first year of marriage was full of bliss, but it is quite the opposite. We lost a child and we lost each other in the process. We fell out of love almost instantly. The romance ended, I guess our marriage ended too. We didn't make any traditions so there won't be any to follow in upcoming years. Happy Anniversary to us.

March 20, 1980

I just got the most exciting news and the most irritating news all in one. Diane just came to me to tell me she was pregnant. I showed so much excitement and encouragement for her until she told me who the father was. This would explain where Nick had been the past few times. She told me it was only three times she was with him and I remember those three nights like yesterday. I am so hurt that my twin sister, my best friend could do this to me. I kicked her out of my home and didn't want to speak to her again.

April 20, 1980

I called Diane to see if Nick knew he was going to be a father. She hadn't told him yet. I asked her to come over and talk to me. I missed her; I still loved her. I am mad as hell at her, but right now I know she needed me and I want to be there for her. We talked for a while before I had her call Nick at work and we made it look like I didn't know about it. Nick was not happy. Diane told me she wanted to abort it until I told her the story of my miscarriage that she didn't know about and she changed her mind, but asked then if I wanted her baby. I knew Nick probably wouldn't like that idea, but I didn't care, I wanted to be a mother and Diane was giving that to me.

The journal went on the next 8 months talking about Diane's pregnancy. She was in school for Criminal Justice and Law and did it all pregnant knowing it would pass soon. The first kick, watching the baby move around in the belly, the birthing classes, Debbie was there for it all. Nick was not. He did tell his parents that Debbie's sister was pregnant and they were adopting her baby. They didn't show too much emotion.

December 25, 1980

Diane's water broke today. We both hoped she would be here before Christmas but, this baby has decided on what day she wanted her birthday to be. Since the day was getting closer Diane had been sleeping at my house. Early Christmas morning Diane came into my bedroom to tell me she needed to go to the hospital. I nudged Nick in the back to get up to drive us. He wasn't very happy about that, but he took us. We weren't at the hospital for very long before Diane started pushing and shortly after that she was born. Our beautiful 7pounds 5-ounce Jade. She had dark brown peach fuzz hair. She was so precious. Diane did such a wonderful job, but soon after Jade was born, she turned her head and wished for the nurses to hand her over to me. I knew Diane was crying. I tried to console her but she promised me they were tears of happiness, so I went back to holding my baby. One day you will know the truth my sweet Jade, and I will be the one to tell you. I made a promise with your aunt Diane that this is how it will be. Your grandma Greer came to see you. She knows the truth too, that Diane is your real mother. She is a very happy grandma, and she has spoiled you rotten. Your grandma and grandpa Elcup have already opened a bank account for you with quite a bit of money in it.

January 18, 1981

This day was a beautiful day. You were christened into our family. You wore a long white dress and you had a bonnet on your head. Your grandma Greer and your grandma and grandpa Elcup came to this beautiful event. I didn't care either way if you had this done or not, but the Elcup side really wanted this and no better way than in their Catholic religion. When you are older and can decide on your own, you may choose the path that is best for you.

March 11, 1981

My mom died today. It was like losing my dad all over again. The heartache I feel inside. I am sure Diane feels the same way. This time I am not pregnant or planning a wedding so my hormones aren't all over the place. I am very sad she won't be here to watch Jade grow up. Please watch over us momma and tell daddy hi. I love you.

March 17, 1981

Today was my mom's funeral. Two years and a month after the love of her life died. A lot of people would kill to have a love like theirs. Now they can be reunited in heaven and watch over us. It was a sad, sad day watching the coffin lower into the ground. The music played were sweet melodies and the flowers were beautiful. Rest in peace mom. I will miss you; I will never forget you.

PORCELAIN JADE'S ESCAPE

Days went on, into years. The first things were written down in Jade's baby book. Jade's first tooth, first word, the first time she crawled, stood up and walked. Her first year, cake all over her face, all her presents. Her second year where she was an early developer in talking complete sentences. The joy she brought to Debbie and the joy Diane had to be a part of her life still.

June 16, 1981

Today Jade was sworn in as my daughter. After adoption we had to wait six months. In this case it could be because the real mother has that amount of time to change her mind. I knew Diane wouldn't change her mind on this one, so today you are All Mine and I love you.

PORCELAIN JADE'S ESCAPE

August 9, 1981

Nick still comes home late, but he comes home. I haven't seen him home before 11:30. When he gets home, he reeks of alcohol. Pretty sure he has been at the bar. Should I be happy when he is here or happier when he is gone?

December 14, 1981

I met a guy at the supermarket. My bag ripped open and my groceries went all over the parking lot. He helped me get everything picked up and went inside to get a new bag. He was nice, handsome and definitely charming. I know I shouldn't have but I gave him my number. He knows I am married but didn't care. We started seeing each other. He would come over about 730 at night, we would eat dinner and play with Jade and before he went home, sometimes, we would have sex. Nick doesn't seem to care to be home with us and my needs aren't being met, that makes me a horrible person I know but, should I really care?

PORCELAIN JADE'S ESCAPE

December 25, 1981

Jade turned the big 'One' today. It is much more fun having a birthday party just for her than it is to have Christmas. I'm sure when she is older, she might not agree. Nick is here usually on Christmas morning, but he is totally checked out. Happy birthday baby girl. Mommy loves you.

January 18, 1982

The pregnancy test is positive. Boy, was I surprised thinking I couldn't have kids after my miscarriage at nineteen. I know for a fact it isn't Nicks. Now what. I don't want any more added drama in my life even though I created some of it. I am going to call things off with Frederick. He doesn't need to know he is the father. I raised Jade by myself, I can raise this one too. I will convince Nick to be the father, unfortunately not a very good one.

February 14, 1982

I gave Nick a Valentines' present letting him know I was pregnant and he wasn't the father. Obviously, he already knew that. He played along with the charade to fool his parents so the funds could keep coming in. He wasn't very happy about it, but lately now a days there isn't anything I could do to make him happy, so I don't care.

May 22, 1982

I get to see what I am having today, if this baby cooperates. Diane came with me. It has been a neat experience so far being pregnant. I can't wait to meet my little one. The doctor came in and did the ultrasound. She took measurements of the arms, legs and head. She checked the face, looking for cleft lip and then had to wiggle the baby a little bit to open its legs. It's a girl. I cried, Diane cried, we were both excited.

August 27, 1982

Nick and I went on a shopping spree to decorate for the baby's room. I couldn't believe he even came with, but I did need his help with heavy things. Nicks parents sent over a large amount of money to spend on the little one. We bought a crib, clothes, diapers, swing, bouncer, bottles...pretty much all you could think of for a baby. I did not need a shower. Who would come anyways?

September 25, 1982

My contractions were pretty bad, hurtful and very close. I went to the hospital and they sent me back home. They were only Braxton hicks. All this is new to me. I thought for sure I was having a baby tonight, but happy you aren't here yet, because that would be a little early.

PORCELAIN JADE'S ESCAPE

October 17, 1982

It was a long labor. Some women have their babies in a short time but I have been here since 1:55 in the morning and I am only dilated to a four. My contractions were very close together but I wasn't progressing. They broke my water at 10:10 in the morning and it has gone by a little quicker but you are still not here. I remembered being here when Jade was born, watching Diane go through all of this. I was glad it wasn't me, but I am glad it is me now. I was so excited to meet you. At 9:33 PM you joined this family. You had blonde hair, blue eyes. you were 6 pounds 6 ounces and 19 ½ inches long. You were a tiny thing, but you couldn't tell by the look of my belly. You are already so beautiful and so loved.

October 18, 1982

Today you came home from the hospital. Your dad Nick drove us home but immediately left afterwards. Your sister Jade was so happy to see you. She loved you instantly, you were her new baby doll. Diane stayed about a week to help us adjust. We loved her being here with us. I promise I will do all I can to protect you. I am sorry your dad doesn't feel the same. I will update all your firsts in your baby book.

I haven't been in here a lot. Not much to write down. All the things the girls have done are in their own books with pictures, most are stored away in a box. Nick has started his staying out late again sometimes not coming home at all. I followed him a couple times in the beginning and I am hurt from what I saw.

1987

Nick has been seeing a lady with long auburn hair. She is quite pretty. I wonder how long this will last for her before he turns on her for another woman. I kept following him each night he would go out, which was almost always. Diane stayed with the kids for a little while. I wanted to find out all I could about her. I wasn't even sure if I needed a reason to, I just did. I took pictures of her and the vehicle she drove including the license plate. I tried to find her name, then, when Nick was (what I thought was done with her) I started following her around for a little bit so I could see the kind of life she lived. She worked at an auto parts store and one day I walked in and saw her nametag, Sally. I said to her "Sally Richardson?" I obviously made up a last name.

She looked at me; "No, Sally Mitchell."

"My mistake. I am so sorry. You just look like a friend of mine and I haven't seen her in a while."

"You're fine." She spoke.

I think I will use that line if I need to do this again. I went home, it was late. Diane always had work to do and had her computer with her. While she was sleeping, I looked up Sally Mitchell and her license plate number. This way I can keep tabs on her. She is twenty-two years old. Nick was twenty-nine.

1989

Nothing happened for quite a while but again two years later, Nick was with another girl. I followed him like before, took pictures of the place she lived and the car she drove. He is getting older, but the women he is seeing is getting younger and still pretty. This girls name was April Jones. She had short curly brown hair. She was nineteen Nick was thirty-one.

"Who is she this time?" I would ask him. He told me to mind my own business and he didn't care what I thought. I honestly do not know what I did to this man to make him hate me so much. He told me he wasn't using his real name with these women. If he didn't care too much, why not at least be honest with them?

1990

This time Nick was with Jennifer Ulisky. She is nineteen. She has long beautiful strawberry blonde hair. Nick was thirty-two.

September 10, 1990

Jacqueline and I went to the store and out for ice-cream. On the way back home, a drunk driver ran a red light and hit my car right where Jacqueline was sitting. I was injured pretty badly and I couldn't help her. We were rushed to the hospital; we were put in separate rooms. I didn't have answers right away and the nurses weren't very friendly about the sensitive subject. I heard from Jade that Jacqueline had died. I was so upset that my ten-year-old daughter had heard this news before me. How was I to protect Jade and her feelings? She surprisingly handled it very well. Nick didn't come around. He was probably out looking for his next life to destroy, not even caring that mine is shattered. Diane helped me get through the pain and heartache. We had her funeral shortly after and that was when Jade lost it. She just realized her best friend was gone and nothing was ever going to be the same again. She cried so hard when they closed the casket. She was lost and I didn't know what else to do for her except hold her. I am going to miss you my dear Jacqueline, I love you.

PORCELAIN JADE'S ESCAPE

December 10, 1990

It has only been two months since you died. It doesn't get any easier. I still refer to you and Jade as my children, like you are still here. How am I supposed to get used to only saying Jade? I still call out to you and when you don't answer I realize all over again why. Christmas and birthdays will never be the same again.

1991

Nick had a lot of events going on with three different women. First, he was with Melissa Cork who was only eighteen, Nick was fifteen years older. She had black hair to the middle of her back. Then there was Frankie Somers who had light brown hair just to her shoulders. She was twenty. Then there was Jill Farnsworth. She had long, light brown hair. She was twenty as well making Nick only thirteen years older. At this same time, he was seeing Jill, I noticed my ring came up missing. I hardly ever wore it so I put it in my jewelry box and now it is gone. It was only my wedding ring, maybe it will mean something better on somebody else's hand.

1992

Nick was still at it. Her name was Meredith Alexson she was twenty-two. She had long brown hair. He was thirty-four. I was beginning to think I was too old for my husband.

1993

Nick had two girls this time. Jessica Newman was eighteen like one of the other girls age before her. She was seventeen years younger than Nick. She had short dark brown hair. Nick was then seeing Natasha Jesby. I wasn't sure what he was saw in Natasha but he found something in her he liked. She had long brown stringy hair and she smoked. She was seventeen. I was in shock to see what kind of charm Nick had on these women; some were poor innocent girls. Nick was too old for them, but he did put on a great face. I feel sorry for these women. They will be used and let go like a dirty ol' rag.

PORCELAIN JADE'S ESCAPE

September 1993

Jade came to me and asked what kind of things would be good to put in a time capsule. Something she could bury for a long time. Her best friend Tilley was putting things inside it too. These silly girls. I wish I would have thought of this when I was their age. I told her to put something she absolutely loved, something she will always remember and I will give her something of a mystery. She ran and grabbed her teddy bear. For some reason this one was special. She didn't play with it daily but she slept with it and every day after she made her bed, she would put this teddy on her bed by all her pillows. I think she really loved this stuffed animal with brown fur and yellow paws because her father won it for her at the fair. She asked me if it would be okay to put a picture inside. I mentioned putting it in an envelope. It was a picture of herself, me and Jacqueline at the beach. We loved that place and tried to go as often as we could. I gave her a necklace with a key on it. I didn't tell her what the key went to but one day she would find out. I have a cedar chest and the key on the necklace will fit it. Inside are all my treasures. My baby's books, little clothes, my wedding album and fun old things I had growing up. Jade will know soon enough all the things I have kept from her all these years and all with good reason. One day I will explain it to her, but today is not that day, so the key will be buried until she is ready to discover it. The real key, the one only I know of is attached with tape at the back of this book. When Nick started staying out late and coming home early, Frederick gave me a key. He told me the house this key belonged to was his grandfathers. It is a run-down house and needed a lot of work, but if I ever needed to get away, if things got too scary with Nick, I could go to this house and stay as long as I needed. There were two bedrooms with a functioning kitchen. His grandfather used to make a lot of porcelain items and sell them around town way back then. He expanded his business and decided to make his kiln bigger and started doing licensed cremations of animals and people. When his grandfather died the house remained empty and throughout time, weather, wind and anything else mother nature could do; it aged. Frederick or his brother Evan didn't want it, but Frederick kept the key. Now it is in my possession. One day Jade might need this. I have never been there. The address was attached with the key.

1994

One year later. He was back at it again. Olivia Trance. She was the only woman he went out with (so far) who was African American. She was very pretty with curly black well-maintained hair. Nick was thirty-six and she was twenty-two. How many more will there be?

1995

Just when I thought things would come to an end, he is out with another one. The youngest so far, the poor lost soul. Her name was Ashley Young and she was sixteen. That is a big difference to thirty-seven. This girl looked desperate for help. I don't think Nick gave her the kind of help she was really needing. She had shoulder length dirty blonde hair.

Every time he was out and not home, (not that I really cared if he were home) but he was out ruining someone else's life. I was his wife, a prisoner you could say, but I chose this I guess, I can't blame anybody but myself. Jade was so young when all this was going on. He should have been here with her. Teaching her and loving her. I had to fill the shoes of a mom and a dad, but there were just some things only a daddy could do, but never did. I wish there was something I could do to make my pain feel better. I wish I could get revenge on all these women who Nick let ruin our lives. They took him away when there were times, I needed him the most.

November 1995

The fighting is getting worse and worse. I cannot take it anymore. Maybe I should move into the house Frederick gave me the key to. Jade should not have to live like this. I should be a better parent to her. If I could teach her anything in this world it would be to always stand up for yourself and believe in the things you can do. Never let anybody tell you different. Love is special. It isn't always like this. I am sorry for the examples I have set and shown you, but my love for you has never and will never change. You are my daughter even from another mother, you fulfilled my heart. You my Fancy will never let me down; I just know it.

Jade finished reading the journal again. Those were the last words her mother said. It was almost like a goodbye letter. Secrets were revealed, things were no longer hidden and Jade knew it all. She took it upon herself to fulfill a wish she thought her mother might like. When Debbie died and Jade saw it all she waited in her room until her dad left then she ran to her mother. On her knees Jade was pleading for her mother to be okay. She hugged her and cried and couldn't believe she was really gone. She grabbed the journal her mother was always writing in and ran to her room and put it in her backpack before dialing the police. That was one thing nobody was going to have. She read it shortly after her mother's death in her own private time. She didn't even want Diane to see it. Once she was done reading it and trying to understand all that was going on, she hid it in the storage shed and waited for it to call her back in. Ten years later Jade opened it and read it again and now that she was older, she knew what she had to do. She lived a life of loneliness and hell with her mother gone. Now she wanted revenge. She was not going to let her mother down.

~ TWO ~
JADE'S WAY OUT

Jade waited in the space below the basement for three days before she crawled out of a secret stone way. There were old branches that hid the ivy vines growing in a wicked twisted way up the house. It looked eerie, but cool, to see this living thing intertwine with each other.

She slid the door sideways and crawled through the brittle branches and untangled herself through the creeping plant. She had planned this day from her very first cremation.

She found the key in the journal attached to an address. Her mother had never made it here and Jade had never heard of this place before but mapped it out and went for a drive alone when she was twenty-four. She enjoyed the scenery. She wondered what kind of place it would be and was curious to even think a town was beyond the twists and turns of Big Rock Candy Mountain, but she found the town just twenty minutes away. She pulled down the dry and desolate dirt road of Scott's Lane and the only house on that road was the one she now had a key to. The yard had several broken down old classic cars with trees everywhere. It was a great place for deer to lay and rest. She pulled into the yard. There wasn't much of a driveway as the house sat sideways. The front door was not facing the road. Jade took her key and opened the door. It led right to a kitchen with an old burning stove that probably still used coal. The water system was plumbed it didn't have an old red pump on the side of the white old fashioned fireclay country sink. The flooring was linoleum, dirty yellow in color. The walls looked like they were bleeding mud, dirt and dust was everywhere. There were two pieces of furniture in the kitchen with white painters' cloths over them. Jade pulled the first one off. Underneath was a beautiful antique China hutch with some ware consisting of plates cups and saucers. The cupboards that had matched the China hutch had dingy glass see-through doors. The second piece of furniture was an oak table just as beautiful as the hutch.

From the kitchen was a short hallway that led to two rooms. The room on the right had no closet. It looked like it had been made as a family room, or a sun room, or even made into a bedroom at one time. The only furniture in it was a tall curio cabinet with glass doors and an old work bench. The walls were also dirty. On the other side of the hall was a bedroom that had the brass bed frames but no mattress. There was an oak secretary desk, a small closet and a small window. The carpet in this house from the hallway to the rooms was very thick and dirty. It had a mixture of browns and yellows.

Jade continued on through the house. She was done with the upstairs; the two rooms and the kitchen were all the space. From the kitchen though, was a door that led downstairs. Jade turned on the light to see if it was safe to enter. She started stepping down each stair and they would creek. She felt like they were going to crumble under her feet. She reached the basement and the only place to go was left and the space that occupied it was a huge brick machine. It looked like an odd portal to another room, but it had a steel roller table attached to it and at the end of the roller was an arched entryway. It definitely looked like an oven; the opening size was no wider than the rollers. It was all brick inside with holes in each brick for the fire to shoot out. The slab inside the oven is what humans or animals lay on to be burned to ashes. Jade was very much intrigued with this. She had never seen one of these but often wondered how they worked. On the wall just across from this beast was a push button and a knob to start and stop it and control the temperature. Jade looked around, she hoped there was more room in here than what met the eye. She noticed a lever inside the oven, she pulled it and the bed plate turned leaving a passage way to what lied beneath it all. Jade grabbed a flashlight and hopped up on rollers and stuck her head through the oven opening and shined her light below. It was dark. There were cobwebs and you could smell the damp dirt and feel the cold creeping out. She wanted to know more so she climbed inside only hoping she would be able to get back out. It was a small drop from the bottom of the bed to floor. She couldn't stand up straight so she bent over and looked around. The place was pretty preserved. The wall to wall was cement but on the one side was a slit. Jade walked over to it and pushed on it trying to get it to move and it slid open like a secret pocket door. Twigs, branches and brown ivy entangled the opening of this secret wall. Some of it weaved in and out of small cracks in the foundation. On the outside you couldn't see much through the thickness of the plant and it was at this very moment; she had a plan and it just had to work.

Jade started by buying cleaning and paint supplies at the Lin's grocery in Richfield, just forty-five minutes away. She spent quite a bit of time fixing up this little house scrubbing down walls and floors, painting, dusting vacuuming. She bought a mattress for the bed frame in the bedroom. By the time she was done it looked like a brand-new house, on the inside anyway. She tried to not be seen by anybody, but she soon realized the more she minded her own business, she wasn't bothered by others. She set out her plan and took some classes on how to paint porcelain doll faces. Turned out she had a natural talent to the art. She learned how to sew and read books on how to run a crematorium. She was ready, all she needed was her first victim.

Each month Jade brought her new victim to the house was a different look. The ivy for instance in the summer time was green and massive growing strong with green leaves all around hiding every crevice. Through the seasons, however, the ivy would taper down, suddenly stop growing but brown crisp leaves remained attached. You could see the wall beneath, but not very clearly.

In November while Jade was not looking for her next victim, she would swing by this house periodically to test her contraption. She had the push button set on a remote that would open the door and the body would be rolled into the primary chamber, but instantly the lever would trigger and the chamber bed would flip. The crematorium could not be turned off by any means. Jade laid on the slab on top of the hopper and she pushed the button with her thumb. The door cleared and inside she rolled triggering the lever and flipping her to the very basement. While the bed flipped a stuffed pillow resembling a body would take the place and burn. When Jade tried this the first time, she had a rude awakening when she flipped so fast and rolled to the cold cement floor, but she didn't care; she knew her plan would work, so she bought pads, pillows, blankets to put down there to soften her fall. All she had to do now, was wait until New Year's Eve 2006, or shortly after.

~ THREE ~
JADE PLAYED EVERYBODY

Jade knew what she was doing all along. She played the victim all too well. Poor young teenage girl who lost her mother. She had revenge on her mind since that age. The questions she would ask her aunt about the case pretending she didn't know much about it or the places they are taking place. She already had the answers. The times she would go see her dad she was already a murderer but knew it. She fooled them all. She knew she would never see the inside of a jail cell.

Jade had a lot of missing details in her story, omitted details was more like it. She remembered going to see her dad and this time she wanted to know about her mother. When they met, where, the story that was supposed to start 'Once Upon a Time' and end with happily ever after. She knew the answers already, but she wanted to see what kind of lie her father would come up with. This time he told the truth.

The time Jade went to classes to learn protection was more peace of mind for Diane than it was for Jade. She didn't need that class. She was the one others should fear, she would still like to know how she daydreamed it all out. It was all common sense to her.

Jade was almost twenty like Diane was when she gave birth. She didn't tell her aunt about her son like Diane never told her about who her real mother was. Jade swore she would never tell her because she knows Diane would try to find him, and where he would be so would Jade be. Any information she had on her son, his birth, his yearly pictures, the things she put in that book by her nightstand, went with her. She will leave no trace.

Jade wanted badly to find the jewelry box and asked Diane to help. Diane didn't want the jewelry box to be found because she knew there was a secret drawer in it and Jade would find it. She knew Jade had a key and it would unlock the secret that she, herself was Jade's true mother. She couldn't face that secret getting out. She couldn't face losing Jade or having Jade hate her at this time. Diane had no intentions to ever telling Jade the truth. When they had lunch and they talked about Debbie, Diane asked Jade if she had found her mother's journal. Jade had it all along and knew all the secrets and answers already. Diane had such blinders on, Jade had her wrapped around her finger.

The shadiest yet important thing Jade did; was found a way into Diane's computer. When they would spend the night sometimes, Jade would sneak in while Diane was sleeping and hack into her computer, another talent so to say Jade had. Another time was when Jade would go to Diane's office. If she wasn't there, she would wait a little bit, but while waiting she would get into the computer to check names and license plates numbers. Some things she had to get more information on, like the ones who married later on in life, she had a trail to follow, but she wouldn't stop until she had what information she needed. She had a hard time containing herself when the evidence of ruins arrived at Diane's office. When she was asked to leave, she left with a smile on her face.

The poem Jade read at her mother's funeral was about what Jade was going to do to not let her down. How can I do what I need to do when you aren't here to do your part. I will accomplish what you have asked of me, things only you and I know. The answers were there all along and nobody listened. How was Jade supposed to move on without her?

As for her father; as much as he should be in prison for the rest of his life, Jade found a way to forgive him and wrote him a letter. She mailed it the day she let Diane think she was missing.

December 31, 2006

Dear Dad,

Thank you for the birthday letter you wrote me. It was the most heartfelt letter I have ever received and by ever, I mean never. I truly believe you meant every word. Sadly, by the time you get this letter I am writing to you I will no longer be alive. I am not sure if you have been following the news about those missing women, if you have you should have known who they were since you were the one who was with them in the past years. I knew all about your affairs, I know all about the heartache you put mom through. You thought you were only hurting her, but you hurt all of us including Jacqueline. I know she isn't your real daughter. I know I am not Debbie's real daughter. You sure have made a mess of things dad. I will not be visiting you any further as this letter will be the last of me, with that said...I want you to know that I forgive you and I love you. The reason why I am saying these things is because of my son. He has forgiven me for giving him up. I knew I would be giving him a better life than the one I could ever imagine if I weren't his mother. He doesn't deserve everything I couldn't give because I never had. Please keep the secret of my son between you and me. Diane doesn't know. I hope when you get out of prison you can make something of your life. I left Diane a key to a house where I did all my work. You can live there, but I am afraid the ghosts might haunt it. I am sorry it has to end this way. Take care of yourself.

Jade

~ FOUR ~
NICK

Not much has been written about Nicholas Elcup. We all know he was a spoiled rich kid who did as his parents demanded. He grew up an only child. He had a sibling for about two weeks but the biological mother wanted him back so Nick lost the only chance he had to have a sibling. His parents gave him everything he wanted, but he had to be good and do as he was told.

Nick followed the rules his parents set for him. He did good in school and college, but as some are away on their own in college, they seem to find some mischief and what his parents didn't know wouldn't hurt him.

His parents owned a lodge in Park City. They visited often during the winter months and as a family they would all go skiing. Nick brought a friend a time or two. When Nick went to the University of Utah, he was able to live in their winter home for the time being. He did do a lot of goofing around, but he also was very serious about his studies and he never let himself get behind. He got his Bachelors degree in Mechanical Engineering.

One day while he was skiing with his friend, he bumped into a very pretty lady and spilled hot chocolate on himself as well as her. When he looked into her eyes, he knew she was going to be his wife. It was love at first sight. They dated, learned about each other and fell in love over and over again. Throughout the months of dating, she had only met his parents once. It was Thanksgiving. Debbie was unsure of herself. She questioned everything she did. She wanted to make a good impression. She wanted so badly for his parents to like her. Thanksgiving Day came and his parents came to Park City for the holiday and of course the snow. They welcomed Debbie into their home and to their table. They asked her questions to get to know her. Where she grew up, how old she was, what her parents were like, what kind of job she had. Debbie answered all of them and had only seen Nick's mom smile a couple times. They talked about the wedding plans and set a budget that of course was all paid by them.

When Debbie found out she was pregnant; Nick was a little afraid to tell his parents. They always believed you should be married first and then start a family. When Nick finally mustered up the courage to tell them, the first thing out of their mouth was, "It's a good thing you are getting married in a few months."

That was their way of being nice, but Nick said back to them; "And what if I didn't?"

And they replied: "You know what we have wanted all along for you. We wanted you to have an education, to meet a girl and date her for a while to see if she is the one for you, then you would ask her for her hand, plan a wedding, get married and start a family. It isn't much to ask for if you want our inheritance. We are sure you could make a living on your own. You could be the Mechanical Engineer you went to school for and she could be the waitress at the corner diner. If that is what you want for your life, then so be it, but you will marry her and stay married to her. When your children are involved in all of this, they will get their separate inheritance, but you will take care of them. We will buy you a house, but you will provide the rest. We can make this as easy or as difficult as it needs to be."

Nick understood where his parents were coming from. They were very wealthy. They wanted what was best for their child, but it now had to be shared with his growing family. This would mean he wouldn't have to work too hard to provide, but he had to keep the promise of staying forever with Debbie. That day he could do it, but something changed. Perhaps it was the thought of being with one woman only, for the rest of his life that he didn't like.

The people Nick worked with were all single. He missed that life, so he just pretended he was too. He would go to the bar almost every night after work with his co-workers. He didn't have a care in the world. He would find girls in the bar and go home with them, it didn't matter where they lived, what they looked like or what they did for a living. Nick wasn't looking for a long-term relationship. This was Nicks secret he could keep from his Mommy, but not his wife.

Every night he would come home, Debbie would ask who he was out with this time. Nick would get upset with her, and being drunk, didn't control his emotions very well and they would fight into the night. He didn't pay any attention to his wife or his daughter. He went down a dark path and let that darkness, that demon grasp him and he couldn't get away, or maybe it was that he didn't want to get away.

The night he killed Debbie; wasn't supposed to happen. He was drunk again, as usual and she nagged him the second he got home. He couldn't take it anymore. There wasn't anything going on in his life that would make him so upset to come home and fight. The alcohol had a lot to do with it he was sure, but he was responsible for his own actions and the time he took his wife's life was the moment he knew just how much he really loved her and how much he was going to miss her.

So now he throws his own pity party in his jail cell. He tried to get away with what he did for just a moment, but the truth caught up to him instantly and he couldn't hide it anymore. He sobered up in prison and became a better person without the outside influence of so-called friends, co-workers or the drink. He was the one alone now. He now understands what he had put Debbie through as he sits on his bed pondering his thoughts, wondering if things could have been different. His parents wont even talk to him and all the money that was promised to him went to his daughter. He threw his life away. Maybe it was just too much pressure and demand his mom and dad put on him. Maybe it was the fact he could fail and would always be a failure in their eyes, so why not just give up and not have a care in the world. Either way he succeeded and now he can't turn back time and do it all over again.

He was told in a therapy session once to learn forgiveness. He knew he wouldn't get the forgiveness he needed from his late wife, probably not even from his daughter and he wasn't sure about his parents, but in the session, he was told to write a letter to them asking for forgiveness and surrender himself to them. One day, he might learn how to forgive himself. He wrote the letters, but he never mailed them. He just tucks them under his pillow every night and he will read them just before going to bed.

Dear Mom and Dad,

It's me, your son. I know I have disappointed you in so many ways. I tried so hard to be the best child you could ever have. I did pretty good for a while. I went to school, I graduated, I met a girl who I fell in love with and I know you didn't think she was good enough for me, but she was so much more. I married her and I had a family. I've marked off the list. I fell into the wrong crowd and I did some things I am not proud of. I ignored my family, including you. A couple things you do not know; Jade is really mine. Debbie and I adopted her from Diane, but I am the real father. You two accepted Jade as your adopted granddaughter the best way you knew how. Jacqueline really isn't mine. Debbie was pregnant with her, but with Frederick and you know who he is. I didn't have a care in the world back then, but I have time to ponder my thoughts and actions and I am sorry for all that I have put you through. If I could go back and change things, I would change the ignorance I showed towards the ones who really loved me. I wouldn't change marrying Debbie, because she truly was the love of my life. She deserved so much better. I wish I could see you again. I miss you. Maybe one day.

Love,

Nicholas

PORCELAIN JADE'S ESCAPE

Dear Jade,

I think I owe you the biggest apology ever. You were so young when all of this happened. You didn't understand what was going on and I wasn't there to help you. I wasn't there to hold you and protect you. I took away the one you loved the most and that's okay that you loved her more than you loved me, I deserve that. I am so sorry I ruined your life. I wish I could start all over again, but as you may someday find out, without the way things happened, I might not ever have you. I love that you come to visit me now that you are older and much wiser, I definitely don't deserve that either, but I want you to know I cherish each time you come and I look forward to another visit. I will always love you and I want what is best for you always.

Love,

Dad

Dear Debbie,

My dearest wife, the love of my life. I lost that in my years and I shouldn't have. You deserved so much more than what I gave you. I got lost in my ways and I destroyed the confidence you ever had in everything including yourself. I am not making excuses for my actions; they were my actions and I am paying the consequence. I am so sorry that I made our daughter grow up without you. I knew how much you loved her. I wish I could love her the same. I am so sorry for not being the husband you thought you married. In the beginning I was head over hills about you. I would do anything for you and then I graduated college, got a great job and met the wrong crowd. I fell into peer pressure. I have done so many things in my life I am not proud of. I can blame my parents all I want, but they aren't to blame. They accepted you in this family. I apologize for them if they have ever upset you. I should have stood up for you. When I killed you, (I am admitting it, I killed you) I wasn't myself. Now that I am in prison and have time to think about you and what we could be today, I just know without the alcohol and all the influences in my life I could have given you a wonderful life. Not a day would go by where I didn't say I love you. I would hold you in my arms every chance I got. I would take walks with you and hold your hand. I would kiss you and never let go, because, Debbie you were everything to me. My regrets are real. I know if I didn't step out with your sister, we wouldn't have Jade. Also if you didn't step out on me, we wouldn't have Jacqueline and who even knows if we would have had children together but we would have each other and I would have made sure that was completely enough for you. I was truly sad when you told me you miscarried. I think if I were to do my life over again, I would have been a good dad. I love you my dear wife, I am sorry it took me so long to see that. Rest in peace till we meet again, if we meet again.

Love,

Your husband

~ FIVE ~
NEW BEGINNING

Jade pondered and pondered how she could make this a fool proof plan. While Diane was making her away across Southern Utah; Jade took a drive to the Crazy Lady Auto car lot in Richfield. She felt like the name suit her very well. She was crazy to do all this, she was crazy to think she could get away with it, she was crazy to think she could live the rest of her life as Evangeline Rose from California. She walked in to the sales office and asked for help with the grey Silverado in the parking lot.

A kind salesman by the name of Timothy helped her and he was in for a treat too, because it was a sure sale and in cash.

"Are you looking for anything specific?" He asked.

"I would like something new. Is this Silverado new? She asked.

"It is new. It just came in today."

"Well then today will be our lucky day." Jade replied, implementing she would be buying this vehicle.

Jade test drove the truck. It ran smooth, it was quiet, it was perfect, just what she was looking for. "I'll take it." she happily said. You could see the smile on Timothy's face.

"We can go back to my office and set up a deal."

"No need. I'll take it as is right now price and all. I will pay in cash."

Timothy has never had anybody pay in cash for as long as he had worked there. "Okay let's get you going out the door."

They went back to the dealership. The papers were typed up for the truck. All Jade had to do was pay and sign her name. She did have one request though; she asked Timothy if she could pay him $1,000 to have the truck delivered to Junction. She would drive her Ford Explorer and Timothy would drive her truck and another salesman or employee would drive their truck to bring Timothy back. They would each get $500 for an hour and a half drive. They jumped at the chance. They followed Jade to the house on Scott's Lane. She paid them and they went on their way. Jade drove her brand-new truck just up the road a little further and parked it in a cow pasture in between bales of hay. She put a large truck cover over it. Nobody knew about it and nobody will know about it, let alone where to look for it. If by chance this truck connected to Jade comes up in any search, she would be long gone by then and her name would be Evangeline Rose.

So, when the coast was clear she climbed through the hole in the wall pushing her way through the ivy and out into the sunshine breathing the fresh crisp air. She slid the stone back in place, looked around and walked through the yard. She walked around the back, under the caution tape that delimited her property. She was cautious as she made her way to the side of her house and up the street to the cows, looking back often to be sure she wasn't followed. You can smell the cow manure a mile away. She uncovered her truck, grabbed the key she left by the wheel well, got in and drove away. She often wondered what her life would be like if she weren't plotting revenge for ten years, but the past was now the past, looking in the rearview mirror was like saying goodbye to the old and looking straight ahead was a new life starting now. She hit the highway in no time, San Diego was her destination. She was going to see her son. Fancy was playing in the background.

WORDS FROM THE AUTHOR

This story was a fun one to write. I received the idea through a dream, but instead of using a journal, the killer would write his victims information down on the wall and then wallpaper over it. I originally wanted to make this all happen in Massachusetts, but thought it would be better if I made this happen in a place more familiar to me.

One day while out practice shooting in the hills of Piute County, amongst the old items people have left behind like a television, bottles, cans, rusted barrels; I found a broken doll face in the dirt. It was fate. I knew this had to be the place where this would all happen. I've been visiting this town (Junction) since I was a little girl. My grandparents lived here. My grandma had information on just about everything. When she died in 2007, my parents moved in next door to her home and my mother now holds the information my grandma had kept.

While writing this story with the inspiration from the cracked doll face; my mind would just explode with ideas and I would just type away with whatever came to my head. To my surprise (in which I didn't know) the house where the women are taken to was real. How would I not know this existed? The interior of the house however remains a mystery. I have never been inside.

After all that has been written and the story coming to a sad end, I really hope that none of this actually does come true. It is just a story.

Thank you, my fans, my friends. You too, inspire me. I am happy you enjoyed the series.

PORCELAIN RUBY
PORCELAIN PERIDOT/SAPPHIRE
PORCELAIN OPAL/TOPAZ
PORCELAIN JADE
PORCELAIN JADE'S ESCAPE